Wanting the Intern: An Age Gap Instalove Romance

Isla Chiu

Published by Isla Chiu, 2024.

WANTING THE INTERN: AN AGE GAP INSTALOVE ROMANCE

First edition. June 13, 2024.

ISBN: 979-8224664054

Written by Isla Chiu.

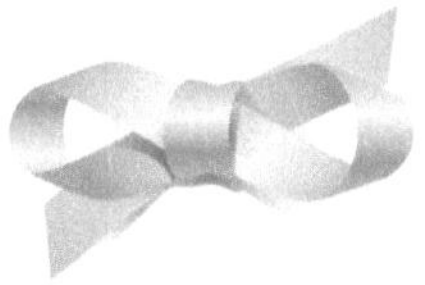

Willow

I LOOK AT PAGE 2 OF the brochure in dismay. The caption under the picture of the dog is supposed to say, "A Shih Tzu named Chloe."

Instead, the caption says, "A Shit Tzu named Chloe."

And I just printed 500 copies of the brochure, each and every single one of them containing that unfortunate caption.

"I am positively and completely screwed," I breathe. How did I miss a typo like that? I swear I read over the brochure at least 200 times. I put my head in my hands. My supervisor is going to strangle me.

If this was the first mistake I made on the job, I would be okay (maybe). However, the brochures are just the newest fuck-up on my never-ending train of mistakes. On my first day, I put regular milk instead of almond milk in a lactose-intolerant client's coffee and somehow broke *two* staplers. The week after that, I spilled soda all over a stack of freshly printed pamphlets and called my supervisor Morgan's wife by his ex-wife's name (in my defense, his ex-wife's name is Mary, and his current wife's name is Maryanne). Just yesterday, I connected my supervisor's Bluetooth headphones to my phone while I was listening to a romance audiobook that was so NSFW (it might or might not have involved a priest doing things that shouldn't be done in a church).

And now Shit Tzu.

I look at my watch. Maybe I can get these brochures reprinted before Morgan comes back from his meeting.

"Hi, Willow!"

I cringe at the high-pitched voice. It's Jessica, an executive assistant (I'm merely a lowly intern) and someone who loves to report to Morgan about every single error I make.

"How did the brochures come out?" she asks.

Before I can lie, *They came out great, but Morgan told me no one can look at them yet,* she grabs a brochure and turns to page 2.

She clicks her tongue. "Chloe, that poor dog." She looks at me, fluttering her thick eyelashes. "Didn't you check these for typos before printing them?"

I sigh. "I did, but obviously, I didn't catch everything." Then I ask, "On a scale of 1 to 10, 10 being absolutely inevitable, how likely is Morgan going to kill me?"

She says in a sugary voice, "8 and a half."

My supervisor comes back from his meeting early. As soon as he enters the office, fucking Jessica practically shoves page 2 of the brochure in his face.

"WILLOW!"

Wincing, I walk to my boss with hunched shoulders. "Hi, sir," I say in a barely audible meek voice, my eyes planted firmly on my scuffed black loafers.

He slaps the brochure. "Do you have vision deficiencies? Because that is the only remotely acceptable excuse for you printing 500 of these brochures with such an obscenity."

"I'm sorry, sir," I say. I don't bother saying, *It won't happen again,* because he and I both know it will happen again—that is, if he doesn't fire me right this second.

He exhales, then grumbles, "I thought people who graduated from Allingham U were supposed to be intelligent."

The words sting. By all accounts, I'm book-smart. I graduated from high school at the top of my class, which helped me earn acceptance to Allingham University, a prestigious school with an acceptance rate of 5% and alumni that include 3 U.S. presidents, 10 senators, 73 Nobel Prize winners, and 35 Pulitzer Prize winners. I also did well in college and graduated summa cum laude.

However, as my father would like to say, my graduating from college with a 4.0 GPA wasn't such an impressive accomplishment since my bachelor's degree in Communications is utterly worthless and I'm ironically a piss-poor communicator (my dad may be an asshole, but he's not wrong on those counts).

Am I any kind of smart besides book-smart? Hell no, if my internship at Jian Marketing Group has been any indication.

"It's almost like you want to get fired, Willow," Morgan says.

Not the first time he's told me that. *No, I'm just an idiot, boss.*

He dismisses me with a wave. "Get out of my sight. Go play a game on your phone, go home, go take a nap—I don't care. Just don't screw anything else up."

Making my voice even meeker and quieter, I ask, "Will I see you here tomorrow...?" *Or are you going to banish me to the realm of the unemployed?*

He rubs his eyes. "I'll see you tomorrow at 9 AM."

I bow my head. "Thank you for giving me another chance. Again, I'm sor—"

He practically snarls, "I told you, get out of my sight."

My supervisor doesn't have to tell me a third time. I dart out of the office before he can change his mind about firing me.

When I'm in the stairwell, I lean my head against the wall. What is wrong with me? In college, I had zero issues pumping out 5000-word typo-free papers on topics like *Heart of Darkness*, ethical journalism, and human communication theories. Yet I'm currently struggling with proofreading brochures?

Before I go home and wallow in my inadequacy, I hit up the kitchen on the second floor, where I will find an abundance of snacks.

I can't help feeling guilty as I fill up my backpack with chips and cookies. Technically, the snacks are supposed to be for clients, but most of Jian Marketing Group's clients are absurdly wealthy people who only eat food from Michelin-star restaurants and/or their private chefs. 99% of them wouldn't even think about touching snacks that you could find at commoner-friendly grocery stores.

I, on the other hand, am a commoner who's trying to minimize her food budget as much as possible so that she can pay off her student loans sometime before she turns into a senior citizen.

"Hmm, either you're a fan of Oreos or you're a snack dealer."

My spine stiffens at the sound of the unfamiliar deep male voice. At least it's not Morgan.

However, when I turn my head, I wish that it was my supervisor.

All color leaves my face as I stare at Adam Jian—as in the Jian of Jian Marketing Group, as in my boss's boss's boss's boss, as in the freaking CEO and owner of the company.

I swallow. Though it's my first time meeting Mr. Jian in person, I immediately recognize his face because it's plastered on posters all over the building. On one occasion (or two or three),

I found myself staring at a poster for a moment too long and thinking, *Damn, who knew CEOs could be so hot?*

Somehow, Mr. Jian is even hotter in person. He has a chiseled jawline that even the most skilled plastic surgeon couldn't recreate along with a chiseled body that his designer black suit highlights exceedingly well. If it weren't for the fine lines around his dark brown eyes and the streaks of gray in his wavy black hair (and the fact that I came across his bio a few dozen times while working at his company), I would think that he was a 20-something guy, not a man in his mid-forties.

My conscience hisses, *For fuck's sake, focus, Willow, and quit drooling over the CEO.*

"Hi, Mr. Jian," I say, trying to act like I'm grabbing snacks for completely legitimate work-related reasons.

He picks up my ID badge, quickening my pulse. "Willow Xu…" He cocks his head. "You do know those snacks are reserved for clients, right?"

I force a smile. "Of course. My supervisor told me that one of his clients was obsessed with Oreos."

He glances at my backpack. "And Pringles?"

"Yep," I say, hating how squeaky the word comes out.

He takes a large step toward me. My mouth goes dry. Our chests are now a mere handful of inches away from colliding. From his height of over 6 feet, he looks down at me (who is barely 5 feet tall).

"Well, you better get going then before the client starts complaining of hunger," he says.

My shoulders sag in relief. "Yeah, I don't want to keep them waiting." Then I notice his fingers, which are still wrapped around my ID badge. "Um, Mr. Jian, you're still holding my badge."

He doesn't drop it immediately. "So I am."

I blink. "Uh, sir, may you let go of my badge?"

A lengthy pause. Then finally, he lets the badge fall from his hand. "Have a good evening, Willow."

"Thank you. You have a good evening as well, sir."

I rush to the stairwell like I have to give a client these snacks ASAP. Though I'm grateful that the CEO seemed to believe me, I feel uneasy when I recall the encounter. Is it just me or was Mr. Jian acting strange as hell? Maybe millionaire CEOs are just like that.

I pat my stuffed backpack, glad that he let me walk away with the snacks, which will likely end up being my dinner. I know I should cook like a real adult, but fresh produce and meat are so expensive, and my cooking skills don't go far beyond making a few scrambled eggs.

My whole body cringes when I think of the brochures and Morgan. My supervisor must hate my guts, and I don't blame him. Tomorrow is a fresh start; I will prove to him that I'm capable of being a competent employee.

The voice of my inner pessimist says, *Or you will give him further proof that you're the worst intern in the world.*

Adam

I STARE AT THE BACK of the intern as she dashes into the stairwell. Yeah, she definitely isn't taking those snacks to a client. I would bet my 8-figure salary that she'll be putting the chips and cookies in her cupboard as soon as she gets home.

Willow Xu–the name sounds familiar. Then I remember one of the managers Morgan bitching about his "nightmare of an intern." Apparently, she was responsible for the loud flatulence of a lactose-intolerant client, which caused said lactose-intolerant client to have an outburst that was equal parts mortified and angry. The intern also put a dent in Morgan's pocket when she accidentally called his third wife by his second wife's name, which forced Morgan to placate his wife with an expensive tennis bracelet.

Morgan neglected to mention that his intern is fucking gorgeous.

My cock twitches when I think of Willow's plump pink lips, the curves hidden under her white blouse and black pencil skirt, and that luscious black hair that I was itching to tangle my fingers in. If we weren't in the workplace and she wasn't my subordinate, I would've asked for her number, then done everything to ensure that she came to my bed and stayed there. An involuntary possessive growl escapes my lips at the thought of her pretty little ass in my bedroom.

I shake my head, reminding myself of the work waiting for me at my desk. I shouldn't be wasting time lusting after the intern. Though I've been called an asshole boss by many, I've never been called an inappropriate one, and I plan to keep it that way.

When I return to the top floor, my secretary Josie says, "Hi, Adam. Your father is waiting for you inside."

"*What?*" I ask, surprised. Baba has never come to my workplace despite me inviting him to have lunch with me in the cafeteria on multiple occasions. "I don't want to bother you at work," he would always say (however, my father has no issue with calling me several times a day during work hours to ask me important questions like "How do you turn on subtitles on the Viki app?" and "Who is this Uncle Roger man?").

"He says it's something important," Josie says.

Dread makes my blood run cold. *Something important*—when it comes to my father, "important" is usually a synonym for "terrible."

"Thank you, Josie," I say, attempting to maintain the appearance of calm. I think I mostly succeed.

When I walk into my office, I see Baba sitting on the sofa. "Hello, Adam," he says, smiling.

I try to relax. He wouldn't be smiling if he was preparing to deliver me terrible news, right? "Hi, Baba. Do you want something to drink?"

He waves his hand. "Your secretary already offered."

I sit on the couch across from him. "So what's going on? Did you need help turning on simplified Chinese subtitles on Viki again?" I would be annoyed if that were the case because I've shown him how to do it 10 times already, but my relief would far outweigh my annoyance.

"Well, I do need help with that, but I've come to talk to you about something else."

The dread becomes a cold hard rock in the pit of my stomach. "Okay, what is it?"

"I'm dying."

Panic throbs under my skin. "What do you mean, you're dying?" I ask. I search my father's face for signs of the Grim Reaper's impending arrival. He looks his age of 72 years old, but he looks healthy. There's color in his face, he has a full head of hair, his brown eyes are lively, and his slightly plump body is proof of a hearty but well-balanced diet.

He shrugs. How can he be so casual about his upcoming death? "The doctor says I have prostate cancer."

"Isn't that supposed to be one of the more curable cancers?"

He gives another maddening shrug. "Not the kind I got diagnosed with."

I grip the arm of the sofa until my knuckles turn white. "Did you get a second opinion? Maybe your doctor is a fucking moron–"

He cuts me off, "I got several opinions, Adam. I've made peace with it. I've lived a long enough life." He sighs, sounding wistful. "And soon, I'll be joining your mother."

When I was 2, my mother passed away due to an aneurysm, so I never got to really know her, but based on what my father and other relatives have told me, she was a great woman with a big heart.

"But I haven't made peace with it, Baba," I say through gritted teeth. I feel like I should be bursting into tears right now because what kind of heartless bastard remains dry-eyed when he hears his dad has cancer? However, my sadness usually manifests itself as anger, so I haven't cried in years. I wonder if it's something I should discuss with a therapist.

He pats my hand. "It's okay, son. The doctor said I still have some time left."

"How can you be so calm about this?"

"It's all of the meditation."

I have to actively stop myself from rolling my eyes. On more than one occasion, my dad has delivered lectures extolling the virtues of meditation. On more than one occasion, I've ignored him. "What do you want to do in the next few weeks? We'll do whatever you want." I'll take a few weeks, months off from work. I have more than enough money to retire because I spent the past few decades busting my ass to attain multimillionaire status. Guilt strikes me. Because I spent the past few decades working so much, I didn't spend as much time with my father as I perhaps should have.

"Well, I do want one thing, but you might roll your eyes if I mention it…"

I hold his hand. "I promise I won't roll my eyes."

"I want to see my son happily married…"

My eyes twitch with the desire to move up toward the heavens. But I promised my father—my *dying* father—that I wouldn't roll my eyes.

Even though I really, really, *really* want to.

It is far from the first time that my dad has expressed his wish for me to become a husband. Like many Chinese men of his age, he wants to see his son pass on the family name, and that means getting married and having children. And like many men my age,

I've prioritized my career over my love life. At one point, Baba got so frustrated with my workaholic ways that he exclaimed, "Aiyah, don't you know there's more to life than work?! Also, working too much makes your sperm go bad!"

Trying to make my tone sound gentle instead of annoyed, I say, "I don't even have a girlfriend."

"I know that," he says with a sniff. "But my friend told me about this matchmaker–"

"I'm not doing an arranged marriage."

He makes his eyes wide and bright with tears. "Even though your father is on his deathbed?"

"You told me you still have some time left!"

"Not that much time."

For a moment, my opposition to arranged marriage wavers. I did read somewhere that the divorce rate for arranged marriages is much lower than the standard divorce rate. And don't I want to grant my dying father's wish?

But before I agree to meet with a matchmaker, I think of Willow Xu, the pretty intern. The mere thought of her curves causes my dick to stiffen. The second I laid eyes on her, I wanted to see her in my bed.

So why not a marriage bed?

"Give me 48 hours," I say. "If I don't have a bride-to-be by then, I'll meet with the matchmaker."

The tears instantly vanish from his eyes. "What? How are you planning to find a fiancee in 2 days?"

I give him a shrug, which of course, brings an irritated expression to his face. "Don't worry about it."

He strokes his chin. "You promise to meet with the matchmaker?"

"If my plan doesn't work out, I promise on Mother's grave that I will meet with the matchmaker."

He stares into my eyes, then nods, seemingly satisfied by the sincerity in my gaze. "All right." Then he pulls out his iPad. "Now that that's settled, can you show me again how to turn on Chinese subtitles on Viki? I want to finish *My ID is Gangnam Beauty* before I die."

Willow

I LOOK UP AT THE TALL glass building that contains Jian Marketing Group. It is 8:43 AM, 17 minutes before I'm supposed to start yet another day of my disastrous internship. Though I may be what my supervisor calls "a tornado of incompetence," I am a punctual tornado of incompetence and have always come to work on time.

I close my eyes and chant in my head, *You will do a good job today, you will do a good job today, you will do a good job today.*

After I open my eyes, I enter the building.

"Hi, sir," I greet Morgan with a smile.

My supervisor doesn't return my smile. "Hi, Willow," he says in a flat voice. "Mr. Jian wants to see you in his office."

I blink, thinking I heard him wrong. "Um, what?"

Then I hear Jessica's high-pitched voice: "What does the CEO want with *her*?"

Morgan shakes his head. "Frankly, I have no idea." He shoots daggers at me. "What are you still doing here? Mr. Jian said he wants to see you right away."

I feel Jessica's envious eyes and Morgan's curious ones on my back as I walk to the elevator. When I press the button for the top floor, nausea wells up inside me. I'm not delusional; I know there's no reason for Jessica to be jealous of me because there's no way that me having an unexpected meeting with the CEO can mean something good. As an intern, I've only disappointed and never impressed.

Oh God, is this about the snacks? Did he find out that I wasn't taking them to a client after all? Am I going to get fired for taking too many Oreos and Pringles? Fuck, I can't get fired. How am I going to pay my rent without a steady paycheck? Not to mention my student loans, which are accumulating interest every second of every damn day.

By the time the elevator opens up to the top floor, I am on the verge of a panic attack.

Mr. Jian's secretary stares at me, her hazel eyes wide with concern. "Honey, are you all right? You look pale."

"I'm all right." Just drowning under the weight of my debt.

"Do you want something to drink or eat?"

"No, thank you..." I look at the placard on her desk. "Ms. Underwood."

"Oh, you can call me Josie," she says. "And go on right ahead into Adam's office. He'll see you now."

My knees tremble as I walk to my doom.

I suck in a breath when I enter the CEO's office, which is bigger than my apartment and has floor-to-ceiling windows that give a spectacular view of the city. After a moment, I drag my eyes away from the window and look at Mr. Jian—or well, the back of his chair.

When he hasn't turned around for a few seconds, I clear my throat. In a voice as shaky as my knees, I say, "Um, hi, Mr. Jian, my supervisor said you wanted to see me."

At last, he turns his chair. Damn, he looks even hotter than he did yesterday. Does he make sure to look extra good when he fires people? "Hi, Willow. You can call me Adam."

I knit my brow. Does he only fire people when he's on a first-name basis with them? "Okay, Adam."

He stands up, then gestures toward a white leather sofa. "Please take a seat."

When I do as he says, he sits next to me–right next to me. Is it just me or is this inappropriately close?

"So you have a lot of student loan debt," he says.

I raise my eyebrows. "Um, I have some debt." I want to add, *So please don't fire me.*

"You have 144,898 dollars worth of debt."

I gape at him. How the hell does he know the exact number? "Um, yes. I don't understand. Why are we discussing this right now?"

"Do you want to pay it all off?"

I want to reply sarcastically, *No, I want to work until the day I die and still have debt for my kids to pay off.* "Of course."

"Then I have a proposal for you." He exhales. "Yesterday, my father told me that he has been diagnosed with cancer."

"Oh, I'm sorry–"

He waves his hand. "It's all right. He's made peace with it."

But you haven't. However, I leave the words unsaid.

He continues, "My father says he wants to see his only son get married before he dies." Then he looks right into my eyes. "So will you marry me?"

"*What*?!" I squawk.

"If you marry me, I'll pay off your student loan debt. I'll also provide for your living expenses as long as we're married."

"Whoa, whoa, whoa, can we put on the brakes? So you don't want to fire me?"

He frowns. "I'm the CEO. I don't deal with the hiring and firing of interns. However, I would prefer that you not work. As I said, I'll provide for your living expenses when we're married."

When...not if. "Why do you want to marry me?" I ask. I assume that he, as a handsome guy with a large bank account, has no shortage of admirers.

"My father wants me to find a wife, and I find you attractive."

Not quite the most romantic proposal of the century. "Are you serious? This isn't some kind of joke, some sort of elaborate prelude to you firing me?"

"I told you, I don't deal with interns. I'm only dealing with you because I want you as my wife."

Jeez, he sure can make a girl swoon with his words. "But you would prefer that I don't work if we get married?"

"If you really want to continue your internship, you can, but you might be sending your supervisor to an early grave if you do that."

I redden. Apparently, my reputation as the world's worst intern precedes me.

He takes my hand, sending a jolt of electricity to my skin. "But you don't have to work because I'll be taking care of you."

I'm not going to lie, having some sexy rich guy make all of my financial problems disappear and take care of me—the idea sounds appealing as hell.

It also sounds too good to be true.

"Do you expect us to stay married till death do us part or till your father...?" I try to come up with a delicate way of saying "till your father kicks the bucket" and fail.

His jaw tightens. "At least till my father passes away. Maybe a year or two after the..." He closes his eyes, letting out a pained hiss. "After the funeral."

"Adam, I'm sorry–"

He shakes his head. "There's no need for you to apologize. After my father's passing, we'll wait a respectable amount of time to get divorced, and you'll get alimony afterward."

"Oh, you don't need to give me alimony on top of paying off my loans–"

His eyes turn into slits. "You'll get alimony."

Okay, I guess I'll take your money if you insist... "What do you expect me to do as your wife?"

"I expect you to spend a lot of time with my father and be kind to him."

I nearly say, *Of course, I'll be kind to a man dying from cancer! Do you think I'm some kind of monster?* I nod. "What else?"

He grabs my hips, making me gasp. "I want us to consummate the marriage." He draws a line down my pencil skirt, making my blood run hot. "Often."

Adam

I HAD EVERY INTENTION of being a gentleman when I proposed marriage to Willow. I would promise to take care of her financially as long as she was a kind daughter-in-law to my father.

Then I saw her walk into my office with that black pencil skirt covering her shapely ass and that white blouse draped over her fat tits.

And I couldn't stop myself from attaching another string to my proposal.

I watch her suck in a breath when I put my hands on her hips. "I want us to consummate the marriage." I run a finger down her skirt. My dick hardens when I feel her shudder under my touch. "Often." I want to add, *Every single fucking night till your voice turns hoarse from screaming my name.*

She asks with wide eyes, "Often? You mean, like, a few times a week?"

My lizard brain wants to growl, *A few times a day.* Fucking Christ, this woman is threatening to undo every civilized part of me.

"At least once a week," I manage to say without growling even as my lizard brain hisses, *Once a week wouldn't be fucking nearly enough.*

She bites her lip, which almost brings my cock to the point of explosion.

The angel on my shoulder says, *You shouldn't be taking advantage of her like this.* I grind my teeth. Though the angel possesses an annoying as hell voice, it's right. Before I can say, *Never mind*, and offer an apology, she says:

"All right."

As soon as the two words escape her mouth, I pull her onto my lap, right on top of my erection.

Her voice reaching a higher pitch, she asks, "Wait, you want to have sex right now?"

If I were a decent man, I would tell her no.

Because I am not, I tell her, "Yes."

I can feel her turn hot with embarrassment as I hold her. Then she whispers, "Okay."

That's all my lizard brain needs to hear before I grab the back of her head and kiss her. I close my eyes, relishing her sweet taste. She tastes like matcha and sugar.

I push my tongue between her lips, and she opens up for me, letting me explore every inch of her perfect mouth.

When I yank down the zipper on her skirt, she catches her breath. I let out a low grunt at the sight of her black panties. Though I'm fucking aching with the desire to tear her underwear to shreds and shove my dick inside her, I force myself to be still for a moment. Willow is my future wife, and as my future wife, she deserves–needs–to be shown that I can and will make the consummation of our marriage damn good.

I slide two digits under the hem of her panties. Her mouth falls open with a moan when I slip my fingers into her slit.

"You like that, Willow?" I murmur. She lets out a louder moan when my fingertips discover her clit. Hearing her groan for me makes my cock grow even thicker with lust and even more eager to find out what being inside her pussy is like.

I rub her clit, increasing the pace and pressure till she's wet and writhing. Once my hand is covered in her juices, I pull down her panties. A possessive snarl climbs out of my throat as I lay my eyes on her pink pussy, which is perfect just like the rest of her. In my haste to bare my dick, I break the zipper on my pants. Oh well, I'll have to ask Josie to get me another pair.

I move toward Willow, but before I can pump my cock into her sex, she pushes on my chest and breathes, "Wait."

"Something wrong?" I ask, trying to not sound impatient (and kind of–all right, *definitely*–failing).

"Shouldn't you put on a condom first?"

I blink. Goddamn, was I really going to come inside her without any protection?

A little voice inside me says, *Well, your dad would be beyond happy to have a grandchild.*

Christ, what is wrong with me? It's one thing to marry a woman I just met; it's certainly another to have a baby with her.

However, I'm not going to lie. The idea of knocking up Willow sends a new wave of hard arousal to my penis.

"Oh, sorry," I say. "I'll get a condom from my desk." For years, I've kept a solitary emergency condom in my office, but since I've been too busy burying myself in work to have sexual relations with women, the condom has always stayed unused.

My dick aches with impatience when I get up to fetch the condom from my desk. As I race back to Willow on the sofa, I rip the packet open and roll the condom over my erection. Once I have my soon-to-be bride back in my arms, I ease my cock into her pussy. Her groans fill my ears as my prick ventures deeper inside her cunt.

"How do you like having your future husband's cock inside you?" I hiss, pumping in and out of her.

"I like it," she whispers, putting her hands on my back. A thrill of satisfaction comes over me when I feel her nails sink into my flesh.

With my teeth, I undo the buttons on her blouse, pleasure filling me at the sight of the white lace bra containing her breasts. I lower my head and lick her cleavage, drawing more groans from her. Her groans turn louder–thank Christ the walls of my office are soundproof–when I push down her bra cups and take one of her hard nipples in my mouth. As I kiss and taste her flesh, her cunt grips my dick like a vise, prompting me to grunt against her breasts.

Cursing under my breath, I spill my seed inside the condom, shuddering on top of her as I come. I'm about to ask if she came too–if she answers no, I'll eat her pussy out until she's screaming my name–when I spot the bright red blood on the white leather sofa. My eyes bulge out of my skull when I also see a little blood on her thighs. Fuck, was I too rough on her? For a second, I'm fully ready to drive her to the hospital and break several traffic laws in the process.

Then a more obvious explanation comes to me.

"Are...were you a virgin?" I ask.

Her face turns beet-red. "Um, yes." Then she spots the fresh red stain on the sofa and gasps. "Oh my God, I ruined your couch. I'm sorry–"

"Never mind about the couch. I can get a new one. Why didn't you tell me you were a virgin?" I feel like an asshole. Well,

I feel like more of one since I'm an asshole for taking advantage of her regardless of the state of her hymen.

She sighs. "I don't know...maybe because some guys don't like the idea of having sex with virgins."

You're wrong about that. I feel an undeniable burst of pleasure at the thought of being her first and only.

"Are you feeling sore?" I ask.

"No," she says. When I narrow my eyes at her, she amends her answer: "A little."

I fix her clothes, then mine, though there's nothing that can be done about the broken zipper on my pants. Once she's presentable and I'm semi-presentable, I stand up and scoop her up into my arms.

She says, "Wait, your fly is open."

"The zipper's broken," I say in a flat voice.

"You don't have to carry me."

"You're right. I don't have to, but I want to."

Josie shoots up from her desk as soon as I walk out of my office. She whispers, "Adam, your fly is open."

"I know," I say in a tone of forced breeziness. "I'll get another pair of pants from home."

"But what about your meeting with–?"

"He can wait." It's a meeting with a big client that brings in a lot of money to the firm, but all that's important to me right now is Willow, and everything else might as well not exist.

Willow

I CAN'T BELIEVE ADAM Jian–the freaking CEO–is carrying me in his arms right now. And I *really* can't believe I lost my v-card to him.

The flesh between my thighs throbs. I lied about being only a little sore. On a scale of 1 to 10, I'm probably, like, at least a 6. But the soreness is not quite an unpleasant sensation.

My body heats up at the memory of how I became sore. I thought my first time would be an excruciating, awkward as hell experience. And while it was a bit awkward and a bit painful, I enjoyed myself. My pulse races as I recall Adam kissing my breasts and touching me until I was wet and ready to come.

When we enter an elevator, I say, "Um, I can walk if you're tired of carrying me."

Adam shoots daggers at me. "Are you implying I'm too weak and old to carry you for an extended period of time?"

"Er, no." I stare at his muscular arms. "You're, like, the picture of men's health. You could even be on the cover of the magazine."

He must not think I'm being sincere because the scowl doesn't leave his face.

To my dismay, the elevator stops, and Morgan walks in. With wide eyes, he says, "Oh, hi, Mr. Jian." I can see the vast amount of effort it takes for him to maintain his pleasant tone while addressing me. "Hi, Willow."

"Willow will be taking the rest of the day off," Adam says. "In fact, her internship is terminated as of today."

Morgan can barely contain his glee at hearing that he is at last rid of the worst intern in the world. "Ah, I see. Thank you for informing me." Then he glances down and blushes on his boss's behalf. In a quiet voice, he says, "Uh, sir, your fly appears to be–"

"*I know*," Adam barks.

My former supervisor knits his brow at the sight of Adam's arms around me, clearly itching to ask why the hell is the CEO carrying a lowly intern (now ex-intern).

"We're getting married," Adam says.

The look on my ex-boss's face–priceless. He splutters, "Uh...um, what?"

My fiance–even saying the word in my mind is so strange–says dryly, "Your congratulations would be appreciated."

Morgan manages a smile. "My apologies. Congratulations. May your marriage be a long and happy one."

I suppress a wince, thinking of Adam's dad. Hopefully, our marriage will last for a while, and his father has plenty of time left.

After Adam says goodbye to Morgan and we get off the elevator, I say, "The whole office is going to know about our engagement now." During my brief internship, the only thing Morgan did more than chew me out for my incompetence was gossip about everything and everyone.

Adam raises an eyebrow. "I wasn't planning to keep our marriage a secret."

I shrug it off. Adam will have to see Morgan and the rest of his company again, but I won't.

We get in the back of a black car. After Adam tells his chauffeur to drive to his house–our house now?–he rolls up the partition before slipping a hand under my skirt.

"Does that make the soreness better?" he asks, massaging my sex.

"Yes," I breathe before breaking out into a moan as he kneads away the ache between my legs. I writhe against his lap, making his hand slick with my wet arousal.

While continuing to rub my pussy, he says, "I forgot to ask. Did you come earlier?"

I nod, too busy focusing on the movements of his skilled fingers to give a coherent verbal answer. Before I can try to add, *I wouldn't mind coming again though,* he removes his hand from my flesh and says, "We're home."

I bite my lip, hot and *very* bothered. I'm tempted to drag his hand back to my sex, but I look through the window and suck in a breath. Adam's house is a massive brick mansion that looks like it was ripped straight out of a grand estate in England's countryside. Maybe I should have majored in marketing instead of communications at college.

He lifts me out of the car. When he starts carrying me bridal style, I almost say, *I'm fine with walking.* But I keep my mouth shut because he will most likely take those words as another insult against his manhood.

Inside the house, we go into an elevator. I have to actively keep my jaw from crashing to the ground because *who the hell has a freaking elevator in their house?!* The elevator stops, and the doors open up to a bedroom that's the size of a penthouse apartment.

He sets me down on a California king canopy bed. "Do you need help bathing?"

Is he serious? Between that question and insisting on carrying me everywhere, he's acting like I'm an invalid, like I lost the function of my legs instead of my virginity. "Uh, I'm good with taking a bath on my own. Didn't Josie say you're supposed to have a meeting with someone?"

Ignoring my question, he asks, "Do you need anything?"

His concern for me is sweet, if over the top. "I'm good, thank you. You should go to your meeting."

My words seem to be falling on deaf ears because he says, "We're having dinner with my father tonight. You should rest up beforehand."

I feel a slight ache in my chest at the mention of his dad. How do you behave around a stranger who you know is dying from cancer? How do you cheer him up? Can you cheer him up?

He takes his phone out of his pocket and scowls at the screen. "Sorry, I have to go to a meeting." *Now* he concerns himself with it. "Are you sure you don't need anything?"

I shake my head. "Thank you though." When he steps into the elevator, I exclaim, "Wait!"

He lifts his eyebrows. "You need something?"

"Um, you should change into another pair of pants."

He glances down at his open fly. "Oh, right. Thanks for the reminder."

Is it just me, or does he seem a little scatterbrained for a successful CEO?

After he changes into a pair of pants with a working zipper and asks me another 5 times if I need anything–I have to answer, "No, thank you," each time–he finally leaves to go to his meeting.

I get up to check out his bathroom, which is what I imagine a bathroom at the Ritz to look like. It has a massive bathtub and screams of luxury; there's even a chandelier hanging from the ceiling. God, what would it be like to use a bathroom like this every day? Then I realize I will be using it every day as Adam's future wife.

I turn on the bath, then strip off my clothes. I flush when I see the little streaks of blood on my inner thighs. No longer a virgin and soon to be a wife. Only a few months ago, after consuming a bottle of very cheap wine, I lamented, half-jokingly, half-seriously, "I'm going to die an untouched spinster." Well, I'm no longer going to die a virgin, and I'm going to die as a divorcee if not as a wife.

As I wash myself, I think of my dad. Should I invite him to the wedding? We haven't talked for a few weeks, on account of me believing he's an asshole and of him believing I'm an utter disappointment, but he is my father. For the first 18 years of my life, he fed me and put a roof over my head, and he did it alone. My mom died only a month after I was born; one night when the temperature was freezing and the roads were covered with ice, she lost control of the car and crashed into a tree. Sometimes, I wonder what my dad would have been like if my mother lived. Would he have been less of an asshole, less disapproving of every single thing I did? I swear, I could become a millionaire philanthropist, and he would ask in a snide tone, "How come you're not a billionaire philanthropist?"

Still, I kind of want him to walk me down the aisle. He would do it; he would also probably bitch about every single facet of the wedding and offer unsolicited, unhelpful opinions about how everything could have been done better.

After I finish with my bath, I grab a towel and wrap it around me. Back in the bedroom, I discover a door next to the bathroom. Curious, I push it open...

And discover a damn department store.

I gape, looking around the huge walk-in closet. Surrounding me is an extensive collection of women's clothes including dozens of dresses, pants, blouses, and skirts. There is even an entire wall devoted to shoes. I open one of the drawers and widen my eyes when I see rows of bras and panties.

"What the fuck?" Why does Adam have so much lingerie? Does he like wearing it? I mean, no judgment if he does. You do you, girl–or guy in this case.

Or are these things for past girlfriends...or future mistresses? Jealousy stabs me at the thought. Then I realize we haven't discussed if we're allowed to have extramarital affairs or not. I have no interest in dating another guy, so the matter is moot for me, but I wonder if Adam will want to have a side chick or side chicks, plural. It's not like I'll protest him having affairs–I can't afford to with my student loan debt on the line– but I won't lie, the thought of him sleeping with another woman bothers the hell out of me.

I knit my brow when I check a tag on one of the bras. 36C–my size. Just a coincidence? I look at another bra. Also my size. I check 10 more–all 36C.

I read the tags on several pairs of panties, and they're all in my size. Same with the dresses, shirts, skirts, and shoes. Did Adam buy all of these things for me? He just met me yesterday. And what if I rejected his proposal?

Ha, you have over $100,000 worth of student debt. A lot of people would commit a string of murders for less.

I grab a T-shirt and pants. When I put them on, they fit me absolutely perfectly.

It occurs to me that I should be creeped out. How the hell does he already know all of my sizes? But when I rub the hem of the T-shirt, I turn warm with what is undeniable delight.

"I see you've already found your closet."

Adam stands under the doorway, one corner of his mouth curved up.

"Is this really all for me?" I ask.

"Who else would it be for?" He picks up a tank top, which seems microscopic compared to his tall, muscular frame. "This isn't exactly my size."

"I don't know, I could have the exact same dimensions as your ex-wife."

"I don't have an ex-wife." He pins me against some dresses, making me breathless when he drags a finger down the side of my neck. "Are you still feeling sore?"

When I nod, he pulls down my pants. I groan when he caresses my pussy. I arch my back, leaning into the delicious, soreness-melting touch his hand offers.

"Your panties are getting wet," he murmurs into my ear.

I mewl when he rubs my sex faster, harder. Then he presses my clit, and the ensuing orgasm makes me shudder in his embrace.

I look down, blushing at the big wet spot on my underwear.

He chuckles. "You shouldn't be embarrassed by your husband giving you pleasure." He lets my pants fall to the floor, then picks me up and carries me back to the bed. I'm thinking he wants to have sex with me again, but he says, "You should check your student loan balance."

"Huh?"

"Just check it."

I grab my phone and log into my loan account. "Holy fucking shit," I blurt out when I read my new balance.

$0.00.

"You're welcome," he says after I've stared at the screen in silence for a few moments.

"Oh, sorry, thank you." I feel like a thousand-ton weight has been lifted off my shoulders. I really thought I would be paying off my student loans till my dying breath.

He holds my face, his eyes staring right into mine. "Now you have to marry me."

My pulse races under his palm. I'm really going to be this man's wife.

"Oh, is she my future daughter-in-law?"

I yelp and duck under the comforter when I see the man standing in front of the elevator.

Adam curses under his breath. "You couldn't call first, Baba?"

I gaze at my future father-in-law, shocked by how healthy he looks. He doesn't look like a man dying from cancer, but I guess looks can be deceiving.

He waves his hand. "Since when do I have to call first to visit my only son? Besides, aren't we supposed to have dinner together tonight?"

"At 6," Adam says. "It's only 3."

His father shrugs. "If you really didn't want me to drop by unannounced, you shouldn't have given me the codes to your home security system." He cocks his head at me. "So you're my son's soon to be wife?"

"Yes. Nice to meet you, Mr. Jian." I would get up to shake his hand, but I'm all too aware of how I'm not wearing any pants under the comforter.

"Nice to meet you too... What's your name?"

"Willow Xu."

His eyes light up. "Chinese?" When I nod, he asks, "What part of China is your family from?"

"My parents are from Shijiazhuang."

His eyes light up even more. "I'm from Shijiazhuang too!" He starts talking to me in rapid Mandarin.

"Oh, sorry, I'm not fluent. *Dui bu qi.*"

"Aiyah, your tones are horrible!"

I cringe, having heard those words from my father at least a hundred times. But instead of scolding me for neglecting to properly learn my mother tongue, Adam's dad just laughs. "But it's okay. Good thing my English is better than your Chinese."

I smile. "Much better."

"Do you want tea, Dad?" Adam asks. "I'll ask the housekeeper to make some."

"I can make it myself." Mr. Jian winks. "I'll go back downstairs, and you two can resume whatever you were doing."

Once his dad descends in the elevator, Adam says, "Sorry about that."

"It's okay," I say. Then I add lamely, "Your father seems nice." Ag, what do you say about your future father-in-law who's dying of a terminal illness?

A shadow comes over Adam's face. "Yeah, he's a nice guy."

I put my hand on his, feeling like it's a totally inadequate gesture of comfort. But he doesn't pull away; he grabs my hand and squeezes.

"We should join my dad for tea," he says before scooping me up into his arms.

"Uh, let me put on some pants first," I say when he starts walking toward the elevator.

He blinks, as if only becoming aware of my bare legs just now. "Oh, right," he says, redirecting us to the closet.

I look at the rows of pants, a little overwhelmed by the sheer variety and volume. Damn, Adam must have spent a not-small fortune on clothes for me. "Should I wear something nice for my first official meeting with your dad?" I ask.

Unhelpfully, he replies, "My father won't care."

I'm a firm believer that it is better to overdress than underdress, so I change into a light blue cashmere sweater and matching skirt. I think about wearing a pair of high heels, but I decide it would be far better to wear slightly less nice ballet flats than risk falling on my face in front of my soon-to-be father-in-law.

I finger the cashmere sweater, which has to be the most expensive thing I've ever worn. "Thank you for all of these clothes. You didn't have to get me them."

"You're going to be my wife. I have to take care of you."

I glance around the closet, thinking that no one is obligated to give his future wife (a temporary one at that) a small department store's worth of clothes. "I appreciate it in any case."

When we join Mr. Jian in the dining room downstairs, he says, "Hello, Willow. Would you like some tea?"

He's already pouring a cup of tea before I can answer. "Thank you, Mr. Jian," I say as he places the steaming tea in front of me.

He clicks his tongue. "Call me Baba, please."

"Okay...Baba." The word shouldn't feel so unfamiliar on my tongue, but when I talk to my father (which isn't as often as it should be), I always call him Dad.

"Aiyah, Baba, how much cream and sugar did you put in this?" Adam asks.

I look at the tea. If I didn't know any better, I would think that it's soy milk from the pale complexion.

"Enough to make it taste good," Mr. Jian says. When Adam opens his mouth, his dad continues, "Before you give me a lecture about maintaining a healthy diet, let me tell you that I don't want to spend my remaining time counting calories."

Adam closes his mouth.

"Please try the tea, Willow," Mr. Jian says.

I take a sip, and it takes all of my willpower to not say, *Holy cavities.* I thought I liked my caffeinated drinks sweet, but Adam's dad likes to play Russian roulette with his blood sugar.

"How do you like it?" he asks with an eager grin.

I mirror his grin. "It's great. The sweeter, the better, I always say. Thank you, Mister..." When the grin falls off his face, I amend, "Thank you, Baba."

The corners of his mouth curve right back up. "You're welcome. Want some more?"

I say quickly, "Thank you, but let me savor this cup."

I feel my own blood sugar spike when Mr. Jian chugs his cup of tea like it's cheap beer. As he pours himself another cup, he asks, "So how did you two meet?"

"We met at work," Adam says. Not a lie.

His dad cocks his head. "Forgive me for asking, but how old are you, Willow? Frankly, you seem young enough to be my son's daughter."

"Baba!" my fiance exclaims.

I blush. "23."

"Ah, so you are young enough to be my son's daughter." Mr. Jian wrinkles his nose. "That means you're young enough to be my granddaughter." His voice drops to a whisper. "Are you pregnant?"

"Baba," Adam says again, this time through gritted teeth.

Mr. Jian raises his hands. "What? Just asking."

I let out an awkward laugh. "I'm not pregnant."

Adam shoots daggers at his dad. "Could you be a little less embarrassing?"

"No," Mr. Jian says gleefully.

I gaze at his easy smile in wonder. Even though he is dying from cancer, he is somehow way more cheerful than my father.

He strokes his chin. "Hmm, I'm suddenly craving Panda Express. Can we order that for dinner?"

Adam stares at his dad in disbelief. "But I made reservations for the Green Lotus."

Mr. Jian purses his lips. "Isn't that restaurant supposed to be vegan?"

"It's a Michelin-star restaurant!"

His baba sniffs. "Still, a vegan restaurant can't possibly serve real Chinese food."

Adam rolls his eyes. "And Panda Express serves real Chinese food?"

"I'm fond of their orange chicken." Mr. Jian nudges me. "Willow, would you rather have delicious orange chicken or go to some *vegan* place for dinner?" He says vegan like it's a particularly vile curse word.

"Hmm, I'd go with the real chicken." Who am I to go against my future father-in-law's wishes–especially when there may not be much time left to grant them? A lump forms in my throat when I look at his triumphant face. Though I just met the man, I already feel an awful ache in my chest at the thought of him passing away.

"Do you want another cup of tea?" he asks.

Though my teeth scream at the idea of consuming any more sugar, I say, "Yes please, baba."

Adam

I STARE AT MY FATHER and Willow in wonder as they devour the gummy orange chicken and lukewarm chow mein. I can't believe they actually like the food. I had precisely one bite of the chicken before silently resolving to make myself a sandwich later.

At least they seem to be getting along with each other. The edge of my lips tilts up when he fills up her plate for the fourth time. When Willow looks at the pile of food in dismay, I pat her hand. "Stuffing you with food is one of Baba's ways of showing affection."

"It's true," he says, dropping several more pieces of orange chicken on her plate and refilling her cup with more of his sickeningly sweet tea.

"Thank you, but I think I might literally explode if I take another bite." She covers her mouth as she yawns.

"Are you tired?" Baba asks.

"A little," she says sheepishly. "I think I might head to bed early if you all don't mind."

Feeling my overprotective instincts be unleashed, I ask, "Are you feeling okay? Do you want me to carry you to bed?"

"No, no," she says when I stand up. Just as I wrap my arms around her, she says, "I mean, I'm feeling okay. You don't need to carry me. You should stay here and chat with your dad."

I very reluctantly let my arms fall back to my sides. "Are you sure?"

"I'm sure."

Baba shoots her a smile. "Have a good night, Willow. It was a pleasure to meet you."

She returns his smile. "Good night. It was a pleasure to meet you, Mister...I mean, Baba."

After she goes up in the elevator, my dad says, "I like her. She seems like a nice girl. And you know I'm being sincere because I'm saying it behind her back."

"Yes, I love her." Surprise fills me when the big L-word so easily slips off my tongue. I'm even more surprised to discover that I might mean it though I met Willow only yesterday.

"Wow, you're saying that even though you just met her?"

I blink. "What?"

Baba laughs. "I'm not stupid. I know you, son. You couldn't and wouldn't keep a girlfriend a secret from me for more than a day." The expression on his face turns serious. "You don't have to rush into a wedding because of my condition."

For some reason, the idea of *not* marrying Willow floods my veins with panic. And I realize I don't want to let her go—*ever*.

"I want to marry her," I say. I want to make her *mine*, and I want her to be mine till my last breath.

He looks into my eyes for a moment, then nods to himself. "Well, if you truly want to marry her, you should give her a ring." He pulls a small box out of his pocket and drops it into my hand.

When I open the box, I see the glittering sapphire ring Baba gave to Mama. "Are you sure about giving this to me?"

"Are you sure about Willow?"

"Yes," I say automatically.

"Then I'm sure as well." With a yawn, he gets up. "I should get going."

"You should take one of the guest rooms tonight, Baba."

He sniffs. "Are you implying I'm incapable of driving myself home?"

Instead of answering his question, I tell him, "If you sleep here tonight, I'll get congee with century eggs, youtiao, and egg tarts tomorrow morning."

My dad's eyes sparkle. "Could you also get har gow?"

"Sure."

"And how about some shumai? Ooh, and maybe some chicken feet. I've also been craving sesame balls—"

I growl, "I'll order everything off the dim sum menu, how about that?"

Baba grins. "Then I'll be happy to sleep here tonight."

After I show him to one of the guest rooms, I go up to Willow. When I see her on the bed in a white nightgown, my cock swells against my boxers. Grinding my teeth, I walk toward the bathroom, intending to take one lengthy ice-cold shower.

"Adam?"

I turn around to see Willow sitting up with her eyes wide open. I should do the unselfish thing and encourage her to go back to sleep.

Instead, I go sit on the bed and put her on my lap. "Baba gave me this to give to you."

She gasps as I slip the sapphire on her finger. "Was this the ring he gave to your mom?"

"Yes."

She strokes the ring as if it were a fragile animal. "Are you sure you want to give this to me? We might not be married for very long."

A scowl breaks out across my face. "I want to revise our agreement."

She widens her eyes. "Revise how?"

"I don't want us to get divorced."

Her eyes are on the verge of taking up her entire face. "Like, *ever?*"

I cradle the back of her head. "I want us to stay married. Till death do us part."

"But...But you barely know me."

I grind my erection against her nightgown, drawing a shuddering breath from her. "I know you enough to know that I don't want you to ever leave my side." I pull at her dress, exposing her shoulder. I draw another shuddering breath from her when I press my mouth to her shoulder and suck on the skin.

"Adam..."

"I'll take care of you. Whatever you want, it's yours."

She cups my face. "I want to have a monogamous marriage."

"That goes without saying." My blood simmers when I think of her being in the arms of another man. I could never hurt her, but I would almost certainly kill her would-be lover. "What else?"

She swallows. "I want to have kids."

I smile. "We'll have a dozen if you want."

She laughs. "I was thinking more along the lines of 2 or 3."

I lift her nightgown, revealing her white panties before taking them off. "Want to make the first baby right now?"

She breathes, "Are you serious?"

"My father would love to see his first grandchild." My throat tightens. He might see the birth of our first child, but it's unlikely he'll be able to see them grow up.

As if sensing my melancholy thoughts, Willow gives me a gentle kiss on the lips. "Let's not waste time then."

Lust immediately banishes any sad thoughts from my head. I take off her nightgown, ripping it in the process. Good thing I bought 20 more for her. A possessive grunt climbs out of my throat as I take in her naked breasts. She's fucking perfect, and she's mine.

I lower my head to one of her nipples and lick the stiff tip. She whimpers, arching her back and rubbing her sex against the bulge in my pants. I hiss, unzipping my pants before I end up spilling my seed in my boxers instead of her pussy. More whimpers leave her mouth when I stroke her clit until it's slick with wet heat. Her whimpers become cries as I slide my dick into her sex. I growl, taking pleasure in the fact that her pussy will only ever know my cock.

"Do you like that, wife?" I ask, not caring if she's not legally my wife yet. She belongs to me, and I belong to her, regardless of any papers or a lack thereof.

"Yes, husband." She screams my name as I push my cock further into her pussy.

"*Mine*," I grunt like a caveman as I mark the walls of her sex with my hot white seed. Then her cunt tightens around my cock, and I hiss out her name while spilling ropes of cum into her pussy. Once I've filled her up with my seed, I caress her belly, as if our child is already growing inside her, and vow to cherish her for the rest of my days.

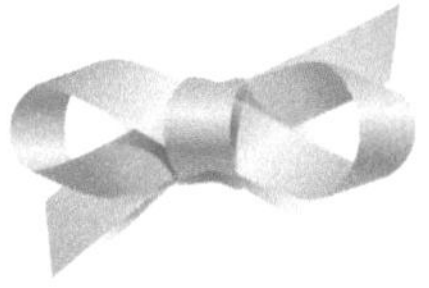

Willow

ONE MONTH LATER

I look at myself in the mirror, unable to suppress a giggle. It's my wedding day today, and I look good in my white lace dress, if I do say so myself.

Under normal circumstances, one would have to wait at least a year to get married at the Pink Jasmine–a fancy hotel that's hosted a few dozen famous pop stars and several presidents–but thanks to Adam's connections and money, we were able to book a wedding here with a mere few weeks' notice.

"You look beautiful."

I spot my father in the corner of the mirror. I decided that I would rather have him walk me down the aisle than not. To my surprise, he's kept his bitching to a minimum. He was definitely perturbed by me getting married to a man I just met–especially when said man was my boss's boss's boss–but his perturbation was soon overcome by Adam's Chinese heritage and massive wealth.

I almost ask, *Are you not going to tell me that these sheer sleeves make my arms look fat or offer some other critical comment about my appearance?* However, I keep my lips closed. No need to start an argument with my dad, and besides, I *know* I look damn good in this dress.

So I say, "Thanks, Dad."

He scratches the back of his head, looking constipated. "I should tell you something."

I wonder if he is going to tell me that these sleeves make my arms look fat, but the door slams open, and Mr. Jian comes running into the room.

"Are you okay, Baba?" I ask, my eyes widening at the beads of sweat dripping down the side of his red face.

He glances at my dad. "I...I just wanted to ask you if you need anything."

Dad glares at Mr. Jian. "Chen, she should know the truth."

"But–"

Ignoring him, my dad tells me, "He's in perfectly fine health. While he does have prostate cancer, it's not the serious kind, and the doctor says he might live for 20 more years, if not more."

"*What*?!" I exclaim. To Mr. Jian: "Have you been lying to us the whole time?"

My dad answers, "No. He did genuinely think he had terminal cancer, but he got a call from the doctor this morning, and she informed him that the lab sent her the wrong test results."

"Why didn't you tell me right away, Baba?"

Again, my dad answers, "Because he didn't want to risk the wedding not happening today." He shoots Mr. Jian a look. "He thinks his son might only be marrying you in order to grant a dying man's wish."

"*What the hell is going on here?*"

I gasp when I see Adam standing under the doorway. I squeak, "You're not supposed to see me before the ceremony, Adam! It's bad luck!"

Adam grabs me before I can go hide behind the mirror. "Like anything could stop me from making you my wife." He narrows my eyes at my dad. "Or anyone."

Dad throws up his hands. "You need to tell your son, Chen!"

Mr. Jian kicks at the floor with a sheepish expression on his face. "Um, the doctor called me this morning..."

Adam turns white. "Did she give you bad news?"

"Well..."

My father curses under his breath. "For God's sake, your dad is perfectly fine! The lab sent his doctor the wrong test results!"

Adam gapes at his dad. "You don't have cancer, Baba?"

"I do have prostate cancer," Mr. Jian says. "But I'm not going to die in a few weeks. More like a few years or so."

My dad says, "More like *20* years or so."

Adam wraps his dad in a tight hug. "That's great news, Baba." Then he scowls. "Why didn't you tell me right away?"

"I don't know, I thought you might cancel the wedding..."

Adam snorts. "Baba, *nothing* is going to stop me from marrying Willow." He pulls me into his arms. "She's the woman I love and the mother of my child."

"WHAT?!" our dads shout in unison.

I swat Adam's arm. "I thought we were going to wait to tell them."

My dad stares at my belly, though I'm not showing a bump yet. "You're pregnant, Willow?"

The edges of my mouth turn up. "Yes, Dad."

In perfect sync that's kind of adorable, our dads jump and shout, "WE'RE GOING TO BE GRANDPAS!"

Adam kisses me. "Come on, let's get this show on the road."

I tease, "That eager to marry me?"

"Yes."

Sign up for my newsletter to get a free book!

GET *In the Dark: An Insta-Love Story* for free if you sign up for my newsletter here[1]. In addition, you'll hear about my new releases and get access to exclusive sales/freebies!

---

1. https://storyoriginapp.com/giveaways/5fbe502e-1570-11eb-a09f-67946e2bdeae

Connect with Me!

THANK YOU SO MUCH FOR reading! <3 If you enjoyed this story, please consider leaving a review.

If you want to connect with me, you can do so via the following platforms.

Goodreads: https://www.goodreads.com/author/show/17011380.Isla_Chiu

Email: islachiu@gmail.com

Don't miss out!

Visit the website below and you can sign up to receive emails whenever Isla Chiu publishes a new book. There's no charge and no obligation.

https://books2read.com/r/B-A-TNDF-UUXLD

Did you love *Wanting the Intern: An Age Gap Instalove Romance*? Then you should read *Obsessed with Her: A Romance Collection*[1] by Isla Chiu!

4 sexy romance stories featuring obsessed heroes who will do anything to have the women they want! Includes *Her Cookies, Blackmailed by the Jerk, Sparks Fly,* and *Alpha Male Blast from the Past.*

HER COOKIES

He wants more than just my cookies. The ramblings of dead philosophers put me to sleep. What doesn't put me to sleep? My very alive, very sexy Intro to Philosophy professor. I have a

---

1. https://books2read.com/u/4DWVnd

2. https://books2read.com/u/4DWVnd

major crush on Professor Newhart, but of course I don't expect it to go anywhere. Because a relationship between a student and a professor? That would be so inappropriate. And I doubt that plain old me would ever catch the eye of the sexy professor.But then he tries my cookies at a bake sale. And soon after, he's determined to also have me for dessert.WORD COUNT: 5,700

BLACKMAILED BY THE JERK

I have a secret.I kind of faked my perfect SAT score to get a full scholarship at Middleson University. It worked, but now I have one major problem—Rick, a wealthy jerk who looks like Zac Efron and who's blackmailing me with my lie. What does the jerk want in exchange for his silence? My body...

SPARKS FLY

Jing doesn't want summer to end. Ryder, her best friend since forever, is going off to college in the fall. Of course, she's happy for him, but she's also already dreading life without him. However, it turns out that Ryder isn't planning for them to go their separate ways. Instead, he's planning to make Jing his.***Celebrate the 4th of July with this sweet and sexy friends-to-lovers story!***WORD COUNT: 7,700

ALPHA MALE BLAST FROM THE PAST

My future used to look so promising. I graduated from high school at the top of my class and got into Princeton. But then I flunked out of the Ivy League school. Now I'm prancing around in a skimpy French maid outfit while waiting on sleazy rich guys at Parisian Dream. Ag, more like Parisian Nightmare.I don't think things could get any worse until I find myself waiting on Gerald Holland, my former best friend. And it turns out he's still a little—okay, very—salty about how I rejected him in high school. But though he acts like he hates me, he also acts like he still wants me...WORD COUNT: 7,300

Also by Isla Chiu

Alpha Male U
Dare
Safe
Professor
Casual

Indecent Proposals
Office Hours: A Student and Professor Story
Loving the Chase
Taken by the Casino Owner

OTT Enterprises
Dear Mr. CEO, I Want You
Dear Mr. CFO, I Hate You
Dear Mr. Counsel, I Need You
Dear Mr. Chairman, I Want to Have Your Baby

Standalone
His Sweet Little Addiction
Just Because of You
A Night with Paradise Four
Taking the Bride
You Equals Mine
Claiming His Runaway Bride
Catching His Thief: A Thanksgiving Insta-Love Story
Kidnapping the Bride
Ringing in the Lunar New Year
The Only One that I Want
The Obsessed Husband
Caught by the Men of the House
Call Me Oppa
Breaking His Rules
Taking Our Bride
Claiming Our Runaway Bride
Sparks Fly: A New Adult Friends to Lovers Romance
Her Cookies: A Student and Teacher Insta-love Story
Quick & Dirty: 3 Stories
Hello, Alpha Male: A Romance 5 Book Bundle
Tempting Him: A Dad's Best Friend Story
His Pretty Prisoner
He Knows What He Wants: A Romance 5 Book Bundle
Her Elegant Prison
Blackmailed by the Jerk
Alpha Male Blast from the Past
Caught in the Act
Compromising the Earl's Daughter

Obsessed with Her: A Romance Collection

Wanting His Student

Claimed on Halloween: A Vampire Romance

His Enchanting Princess

His Lovely Prisoner

My Best Friend Forever

A Werewolf Jock for Thanksgiving

Enchanted by You: A Romance Collection

To Have Her: An Alpha Male Romance Collection

You're Mine, Wife

Her Beautiful Captor: A Captive Romance Collection

His Exquisite Prisoner

My First Theft Went a Little Like This

A Werewolf Jock for the New Year

Taking Back My Bride

So Much More

My Immortal Valentine

Short and Not So Sweet: A Short Story Collection

Caught by Mr. Smith

Bad Habits: A MMF Romance

Claiming Lady Wynn

Compromised: A Romance Collection

Over the Moon(cake) for You

The Sweetest Revenge: An Age Gap Romance

Noticed by My Dad's Best Friend: An Age Gap Romance

Bought by My Best Friend's Dad: An Age Gap Romance

Mile High with My Dad's Best Friend: An Age Gap Romance

Dad's Former Best Friend Just Got Out of Prison: An Age Gap Romance

Bought by My Dad's Boss: An Age Gap Romance

Found by My Bully's Dad: An Age Gap Romance

Wanted by My Best Friend's Dad: An Age Gap Romance
Caught by the King: An Age Gap Romance
Saved by My Professor: An Age Gap Romance
Claimed by a Billionaire on Christmas Eve: An Age Gap
Romance
Bought by My Bully's Dad: An Age Gap Romance
Older Than Me: An Age Gap Romance Collection
Wanted by My Ex-Boyfriend's Dad: An Age Gap Romance
Caught by My Dad's Boss: An Age Gap Romance
A Billionaire for Lunar New Year: An Age Gap Romance
To Be His: An Age Gap Romance Collection
Bought by the Billionaire: An Age Gap Romance
Caught by My Boyfriend's Dad: An Age Gap Romance
Discovered by My Best Friend's Dad: An Age Gap Romance
Caught with the King: An Age Gap Romance
Surprised by the Billionaire: An Age Gap Romance
Wedded to the Mobster: An Age Gap Romance
Noticed by My Boyfriend's Coach: An Age Gap Romance
Picked Up by the Mobster: An Age Gap Romance
Kidnapped by the Billionaire: An Age Gap Romance
Caught by My Professor: An Age Gap Romance
Working for My Dad's Best Friend: An Age Gap Romance
Waiting on My Dad's Former Friend: An Age Gap Romance
Trapped in the Storm With My Boyfriend's Dad: An Age Gap
Romance
She's Mine: An Age Gap Romance Collection
Claimed by the Mountain Man: An Age Gap Romance
An Offer from My Dad's Creditor: An Age Gap Romance
Knocked Up by the Tycoon: An Age Gap Romance
Caught by the College President: An Age Gap Romance
Wanted by My Fake Boyfriend's Dad: An Age Gap Romance

An Offer from the CEO: An Age Gap Romance
Claimed by the Hotel Owner: An Age Gap Romance
Found by the Cowboy: An Age Gap Romance
Claimed by the Lawyer: An Age Gap Romance
Security Risk: An Age Gap Romance
Prom Night with My Boyfriend's Dad: An Age Gap Romance
Trapping the Billionaire: An Age Gap Romance
My Best Friend's Stepbrother: An Age Gap Romance
My Billionaire Ex-Boyfriend
The Mobster's Property: An Age Gap Romance
Pursued by the Club Owner: An Age Gap Romance
He's Obsessed: An Age Gap Romance Collection
Taken by the Senator: An Age Gap Romance
Alpha Male Alert: An Age Gap Romance Collection
Wanting the Intern: An Age Gap Instalove Romance
Noticed by My Bully's Dad: An Age Gap Romance